this
·little·orchard·
book belongs to

....

....

ORCHARD BOOKS
96 Leonard Street, London EC2A 4RH
Orchard Books Australia
14 Mars Road, Lane Cove, NSW 2066
1 86039 492 2 (hardback)
1 86039 484 1 (paperback)
First published in Great Britain in 1997
Copyright © Carol Thompson 1997
The right of Carol Thompson to be identified as the author and illustrator of this work has been
asserted by her in accordance with the Copyright, Designs and Patents Act, 1988.
A CIP catalogue record for this book is available from the British Library.
Printed in Italy

Counting Rhymes

Carol Thompson

• little • orchard •

Two little eyes to look around,
Two little ears to hear each sound,

One little nose to smell what's sweet,
One little mouth that likes to eat.

Baa, baa, black sheep
Have you any wool?
Yes, sir, yes, sir, three bags full;

One for the master, and one for the dame,
And one for the little boy who
lives down the lane.

Five little peas in a pea-pod pressed,
One grew, two grew, and so did all the rest.

They grew and grew and did not stop,
Until one day the pod went POP!

One, two, three, four, five,
Once I caught a fish alive.

Six, seven, eight, nine, ten,
Then I let it go again.

Why did you let it go?
Because it bit my finger so.

Which finger did it bite?
This little finger on the right.

One, two,
buckle my shoe.

Three, four,
knock at the door.

Five, six, pick up sticks.

Seven, eight, lay them straight.

Nine, ten,
a big fat hen.

Five little ladies going for a walk,
Five little ladies stop for a talk.

Along come five little gentlemen,
They all dance together and that makes ten.